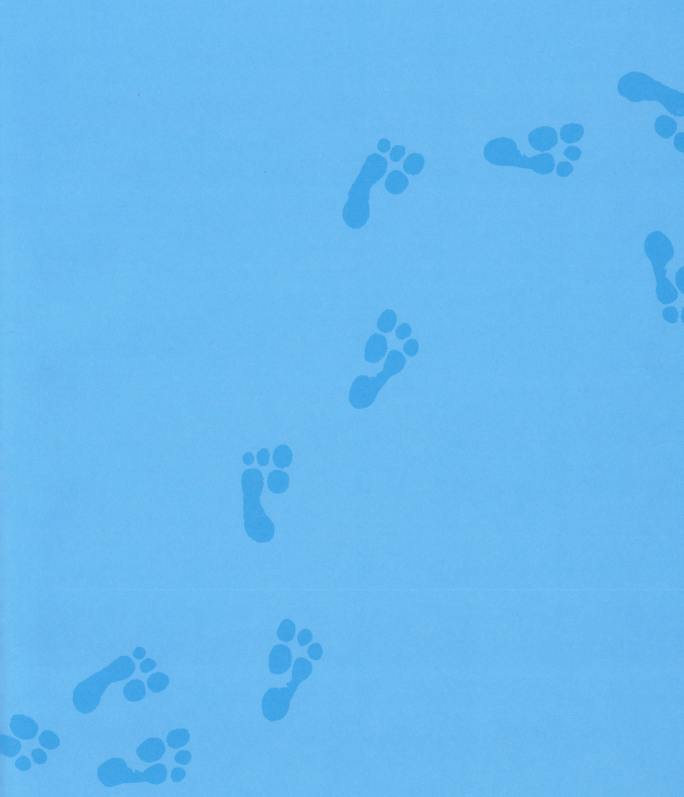

Written by **Lisa Wheeler**   Illustrated by **Chris Van Dusen**

Even MONSTERS Go to SCHOOL

BALZER + BRAY
An Imprint of HarperCollinsPublishers

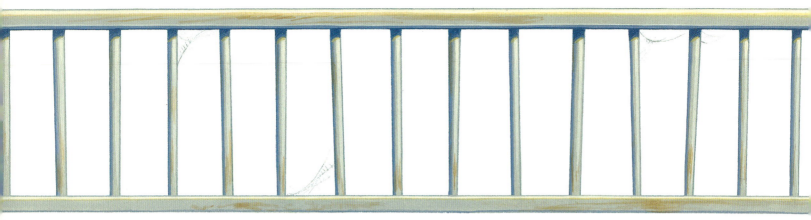

Balzer + Bray is an imprint of HarperCollins Publishers.

Even Monsters Go to School
Text copyright © 2019 by Lisa Wheeler
Illustrations copyright © 2019 by Chris Van Dusen

ISBN 978-0-06-236642-9

The illustrations were done in gouache.
19 20 21 22 23 SCP 10 9 8 7 6 5 4 3 2 1
❖
First Edition
Typography by Dana Fritts

For Erin Wheeler, Sydney Christie, Debbie Case,
Melissa Tkacs, and teachers everywhere.
Thanks for enriching our little monsters.

—L.W.

For Lisa—a whiz with words.

—C.V.D.

When Bigfoot wakes, he combs his hair . . .

and steps out in the morning air.

Yellow bus is waiting there.

Even Bigfoot goes to school.

Frankenstein is clean and neat.
His jacket's new. His shoes are sweet!
He finds a chair and takes a seat.
Even Frankie goes to school.

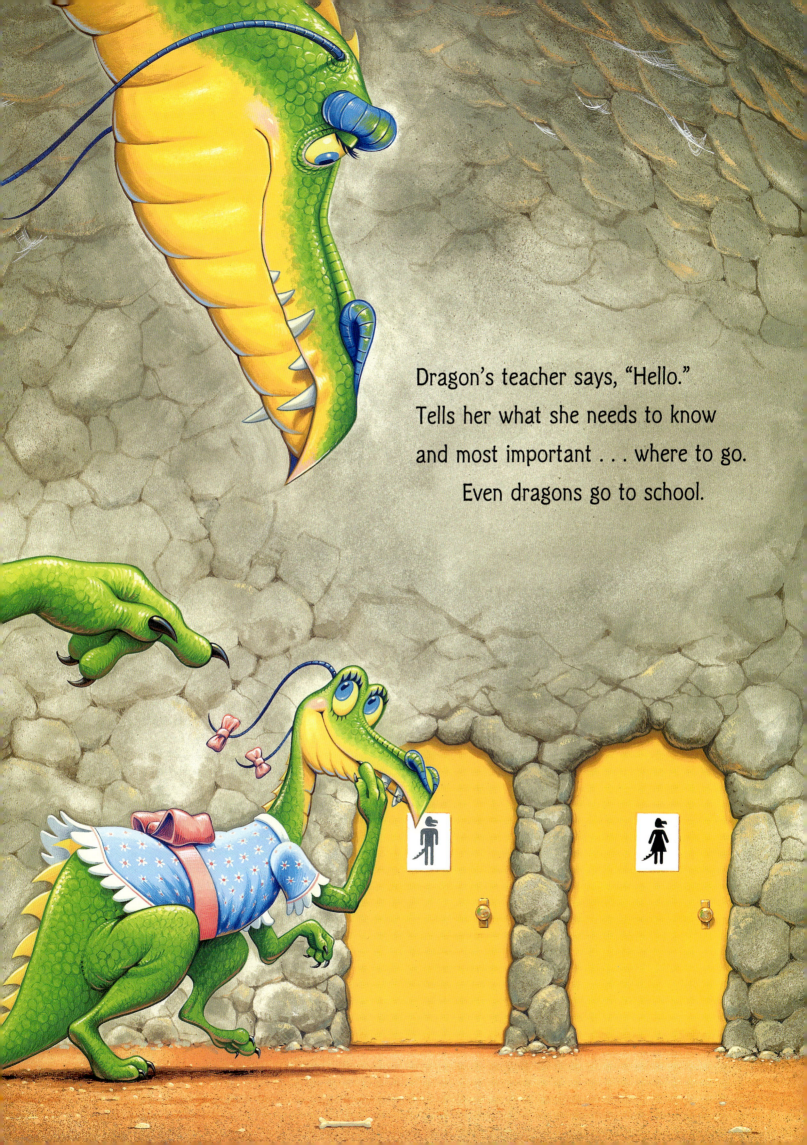

Dragon's teacher says, "Hello."
Tells her what she needs to know
and most important . . . where to go.
Even dragons go to school.

Yeti is a bashful guy.

When making friends he's kind of shy.

Today he smiles and whispers, "Hi."

Even Yeti goes to school.

Troll likes recess in the sun.

Outside voices!

Scream and run!

"Tag! You're it!" He's having fun!
Even bridge trolls go to school.

Loch Ness Monster's favorite time
is learning her first nursery rhyme.
Teacher reads it line by line.
Even Nessie goes to school.

Giant's glad he brought his lunch—
ripe bananas in a bunch
and carrot sticks to *crunch, crunch, crunch!*
Even giants go to school.

Aliens with great big eyes

go gaga over school supplies!

They learn to count in star-filled skies.
Even aliens go to school.

BIKES
ONLY

You brush your teeth.
You feed yourself.

You put your toys back on the shelf.
You're ready! And you know the rule . . .

All little monsters go to school.